The Real Floppy

Roderick Hunt • Alex Brychta

OXFORD
UNIVERSITY PRESS

The children ran onto the sand.

"Let's play here," said Biff.

Wilma threw a ball and
Floppy ran after it.

Floppy ran back with the ball.

Dad ran up. "Stop!" he said.

"Look at that," said Dad.

"Dogs can't go on the sand."

"Poor Floppy!" said Mum.
"I'll take him for a walk."

The children were upset.

They didn't want Floppy to go.

"Let's give Mum a surprise,"
said Dad.

They made a big pile of sand.
Everyone helped.

"Now let's pat it flat," said Dad.

"Let's make his head," said Biff.

"And his ears," said Chip.

"Let's put in his eyes," said Wilf.

"And make his tail," said Kipper.

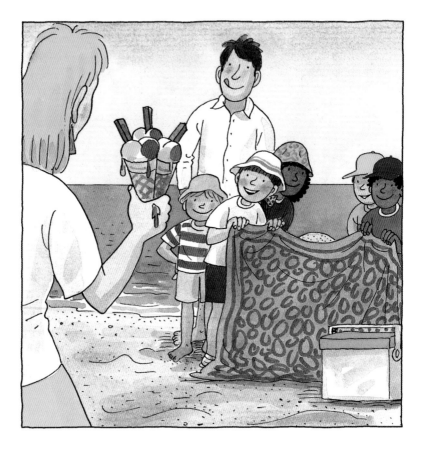

Mum came back.

"Surprise! Surprise!" said Biff.

"A Floppy made of sand!"
said Mum.

"It's a good sand dog,"
said Kipper.
"But I love the real Floppy best."

Think about the story

Why wasn't Floppy allowed on the beach?

What was Mum's surprise? Why was it a good surprise?

Why were the children happy when they were making Mum's surprise?

What have you made out of sand? Were you proud of it?

Picture puzzle

How many things can you find beginning with the same sound as the 's' in sea?

Useful common words repeated in this story and other books at Level 3.

children   his   surprise   let's   make   the   said
Names in this story: Mum   Dad   Biff   Chip   Kipper
Wilf   Wilma   Floppy

(Answer to picture puzzle: sail, sand, sandcastle, sea, sunglasses)